BRATZ™

Jade®

Xtreme Kool!

Used under license by Penguin Young Readers Group.
Published by GROSSET & DUNLAP, a division of
Penguin Young Readers Group, 345 Hudson Street,
New York, NY 10014. GROSSET & DUNLAP is a
trademark of Penguin Group (USA) Inc.
Published simultaneously in Canada. Printed in U.S.A.
ISBN 0-448-43323-0 A B C D E F G H I J

Hey! My name is Jade.!
My fashion passion is clothes that are extreme and far-out! My friends call me "Kool Kat" because I love cats! (And because I'm sooooooo cool!)

Hair We Go!

Thinkin' about a new hairstyle? Here's a list of hair do's and don'ts to think about.

The big don't: Forget about getting the same haircut as your favorite movie star. The best haircut is the one that makes you look your best, not one that makes you look like you're someone else. Be free and XPRESS YOURSELF!

Here's the Hair Do's:

Your hair should highlight what's best about the face it's framing. So before you cut, study your face. Then see which of these looks is best for you.

If your face is oval in shape, you can wear your hair almost any way at all. If you have a diamond shape face with a narrow chin, try wide bangs with a chin-length cut.

If your face is square shaped, make sure your bangs are cut softly and just slightly longer than your temples. Try a short cut that's a little fluffed up on top.

If your face is round, keep the sides of your hair close to your face, and add a little height to the hair on the top of your head.

If you've got a heart-shaped face, try a chin length hairstyle, with some curve or bounce to it. Part your hair on the side and slant your bangs.

Dance Dilemma!

"Wow Jade, that dress is so chic! It makes you look great!" my friend Yasmin gasped as I modeled my new black dress in her living room on the night of the Spring Fling dance at our school.

"Wrong," I told her plainly.

"Huh?" she asked.

"I make the *dress* look funkadelic!" I corrected her.

We both smiled. Yasmin and I both know that real beauty can't be found in a designer dress. It has to come from inside. But great clothes never hurt anyone either, right? Lookin' good means feelin' good!

"I've never seen you wear a plain black dress," Yasmin noted. "You're usually into far-out patterns."

"I know," I said. "I thought I'd try something different tonight."

"Change is good," Yasmin agreed. "How does it feel?"

"A little weird," I admitted.

That was the truth. I kind of missed the funky far-out look I usually went around in. But this was an important dance. I wanted to feel different. And I definitely did. Besides, I wasn't completely without fashion flash and flair. My shoes were covered with sparkly jewels, and my handbag had a silver lightning embroidered across the front.

"Well, you don't look weird; you look great," Yasmin assured me. "I've got to go. I've got to start getting ready, too."

"See ya' at the dance," I said as she left my house.

Just then my cell phone rang. I hurried over and took it from my bag. "Hello?" I said into the receiver. I could feel a smile dash across my face when I heard the voice on the other end. It was my friend Dylan.

"Hey Dylan, what's the good word?" I asked him.

"Not so good," Dylan answered.

My heart skipped a beat. "Are you okay?" I asked.

"I'm okay, but my car's not. It won't start. I have to have it towed to the repair shop."

"Oh no!" I exclaimed. "Will it be ready in time for the dance?"

"I don't think so," he admitted. "But, hey, we can still get there. We'll just have to take the bus."

The bus? That wasn't exactly what I'd had in mind. Still, going to the dance on the bus was better than not going at all. "That's okay," I assured him. "As long as we get there somehow, it doesn't matter to me."

"Gee, you're such a good friend, Jade," Dylan told me.

"I know," I giggled. "You're a lucky guy."

Dylan laughed. "You don't have to tell me that. Look, I'll be at your house in one hour."

"I'll be waiting," I assured him.

As I waited for Dylan to arrive, I looked out the window. The night was clear and cool. That was good. If I was going to be waiting outside for a bus, at least the weather was nice. I couldn't deal with a bad hair night.

Finally, the doorbell rang. I opened the door. . .and gasped. I barely recognized my buddy Dylan. He looked sooooo good in his black tux with a white bow tie, white cummerbund, and a small white rose in his jacket pocket.

"This is for you," he said, as he handed me a small wrist bouquet covered with tiny white rosebuds.

"It's so chic!" I said as I slipped it on.

"Thanks," Dylan replied.

"Well, we'd better get going," he said. "We don't know how long we'll have to wait."

We got to the bus stop just in time to see the bus pulling away.

"Don't worry," I told Dylan. "There'll be another one, soon." I sat down on a white bench near the bus stop, and waited for the next bus. Dylan stood beside me, staring down the street.

It seemed to be taking a long time. Finally, Dylan said, "I think I see a bus," he said.

"Where?" I asked, jumping up and walking in front of him.

"Uh, Jade," Dylan said slowly.

"What?"

"Your dress."

I smiled. "I know, it's really great isn't it?"

"Yeah," Dylan assured me. "But it's. . .it's. . ."

"It's what?"

"It's covered with paint," he said suddenly.

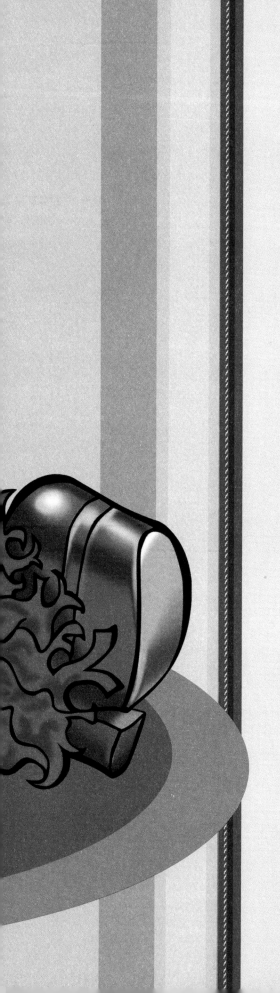

"What?!"

"It's covered in paint on the back," Dylan said. "The bench was just painted. You have white stripes on the back of your dress."

I turned and looked at the bench. There wasn't a "wet paint" sign anywhere…until I looked under the bench. There, on the floor, was a yellow sign that said "Wet Paint."

"Look, if you want to go home and change…" Dylan began.

But there wasn't time for that. The bus was just a few blocks away. If we had to wait for another one, we'd miss the dance all together.
There was only one thing to do.

Quickly I lay face down on the wet bench. Then I rolled over and lay face up.

"What are you doing?" Dylan asked, surprised. "Do you want to put more paint on the dress?"

I nodded. "Sure, why not. Stripes are cool!"

We were so glad to finally get to the dance and meet up with the rest of our friends! We all had a great time dancin' together. Soon, the bandleader was announcing the names of the dance's king and queen and their royal court.

"Do you think we have a chance?" Dylan asked me.

"I don't know," I said. "But I'm having so much fun, it doesn't really matter."

"The first award goes to the bestdressed couple at the dance," the bandleader said into his microphone. "A couple whose look is coordinated, cool, and completely unique. The best- dressed award goes to …Jade and Dylan!"

"Wow!" I squealed as we went up to the stage to get our awards.

"Jade, no one else here has a dress like that," the bandleader said. "Can you tell everyone where you found it?"

"Oh, just laying around," I said, winking at Dylan.

"Who is the designer?" the bandleader asked.

"It's by a new company," I told him, "called Wet Paint."

"Okay girls, remember that name," the bandleader said.
"That's right," I agreed. "I can honestly say that every girl in this room should be on the lookout for Wet Paint."

Then Dylan and I started laughing. Everyone else in the room wondered why. But I'll never tell.
And don't you tell either, 'kay?

Funky Fresh Dress!

Design a totally far-out dress that'll make me stand out from the crowd at the next school dance!

My Secret Stuff

My handbag is soooo funky. I found it at a vintage shop. No one else at the dance is going to have a purse like this one! I'll be unique to the Xtreme!

Unfortunately, the bag is really small. There's not much I can sneak inside, and there's so many things I want to bring along. So I'm leaving it up to you. Here's three things I'm bringing to the prom. Can you think of three more things I should pack for the big night?

Party Time!

I like to party to the Xtreme. But let's face it, some parties are hot, and some are not. Which of these party ideas have real appeal? Rate the party plans from 1 to 5. 1 means time to go home early, and 5 means dance all night!

- ☐ Spa Makeover Party
- ☐ Beach Party
- ☐ Sunset Picnic
- ☐ The Late Movie Show
- ☐ A Skating Party

Now that that's settled, could you create a dazzlin' design that's just right for the party you picked?

These Shoes Got Sole!

You don't need a ton of cash to flash fancy footwear. All you need is a wild imagination, and a pair of old fashioned canvas sneakers!

You will need: A pair of canvas sneakers (any color or brand will work), fabric paints, fabric glue, plastic jewels, white shoe laces, newspaper or a drop cloth.

Here's what you do: Before you paint your sneaks, work out a design that you like. It can be anything—shapes, stars, hearts, or even your favorite Bratz girl's logo. (In my case, that's that Kool Kat you see me with all the time.)

Once you've got your pattern worked out, cover your workspace with newspaper or a drop cloth. Use a pencil or colored chalk to put your pattern on your sneaks. Then paint in your pattern. Use the fabric glue to attach the jewels wherever you'd like.

Use this space to design your shoes.

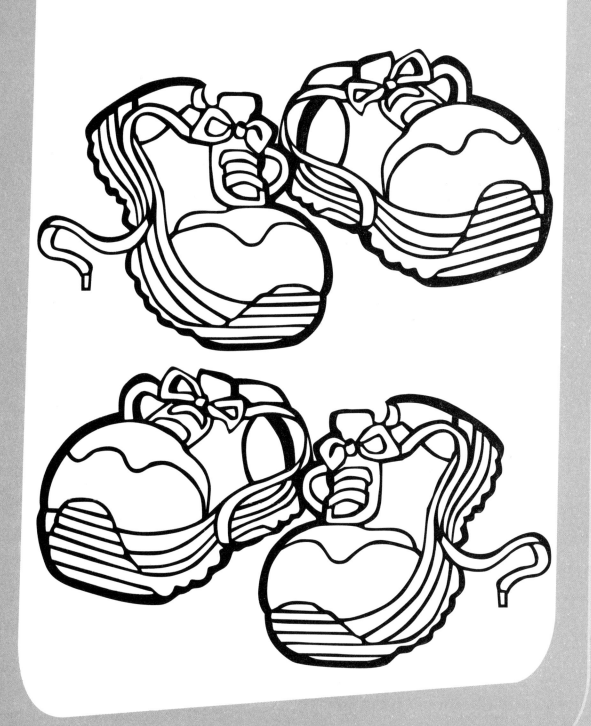

The Eyes Have It!

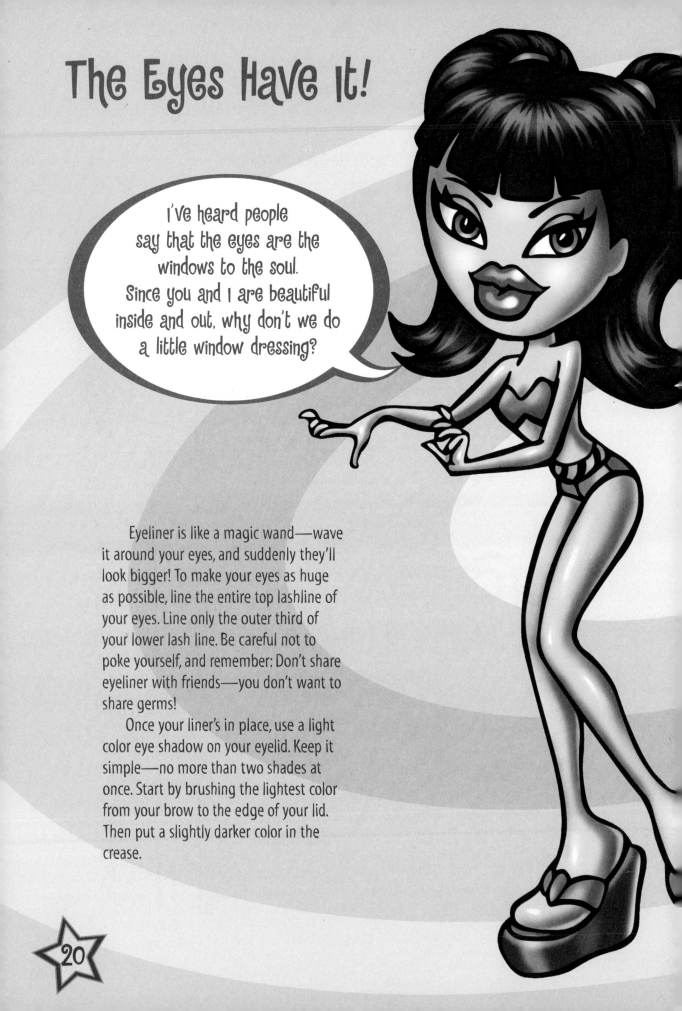

I've heard people say that the eyes are the windows to the soul. Since you and I are beautiful inside and out, why don't we do a little window dressing?

Eyeliner is like a magic wand—wave it around your eyes, and suddenly they'll look bigger! To make your eyes as huge as possible, line the entire top lashline of your eyes. Line only the outer third of your lower lash line. Be careful not to poke yourself, and remember: Don't share eyeliner with friends—you don't want to share germs!

Once your liner's in place, use a light color eye shadow on your eyelid. Keep it simple—no more than two shades at once. Start by brushing the lightest color from your brow to the edge of your lid. Then put a slightly darker color in the crease.

I'm trying to catch the eye of a special guy!
You're a whiz in the eye make-up biz! Can you perform
some make-up magic that'll make him flip his lid?

Diamonds are a Girl's Best Friend . . . But Real Friends Are Pretty Wonderful, Too!

I love wild jewelry—the more far-out the better. I'd love it if you could add a lot of Xtreme sparkle to my look. And while you're at it, maybe you can come up with some baubles for my girls, too.

From Jeans That Drag... To a Far Out Bag!

It's never easy to part with your favorite old pair of jeans if they are too small or totally worn out. So why do it? Instead, cut them up, add a few stitches, and . . . wahoo! You've got a book bag, that's jeans to the X-treme!

Here's how to make your own blue jean book bag.

1. Button and zip the jeans and turn them inside out.

2. Ask an adult to use a pair of fabric shears to cut off the jean legs about three inches from the crotch.

3. Fold the cut off jeans, making sure to match up the side seams.

4. Ask an adult to use a sewing machine to sew each leg opening closed, about one inch from the cut edge.

5. Turn the jeans right side out.

6. To make a handle, thread a cotton belt through the belt loops and tie the ends together.

Xpress Yourself to the Xtreme!

Turn these plain old bags into out-of-sight delights. Let your imagination run wild!

13 43 42 42 23 32 21

15 14 21 15   13 33 14 15!

51 33 43   11 36 15 41 33 41 33

16 11 36   33 43 42.

23 25 32 33 45   51 33 43

45 23 26 26   21 33

45 23 26 14   16 33 36

42 22 23 41 13 33 14 15!

Have no idea what I'm talking about? Just check out the next page to crack the code!

My friends and I have a secret code. We use it whenever we want to send a note—and we don't want anyone else to know what we're writing about. (Hey, you never know who can get their hands on your private notes!) Now we're letting you in on our secret!

To crack the code, use this grid. Each letter on the grid is located in one row and one column. So J would be 24, because it's in the 2 row, and the 4 column. E would be 15, because it's in the 1 row and the 5 column.

Using this code, my name would be written

24 11 14 15.
J A D E

Get it? Now, use the code to figure out what I was talking about!

	1	2	3	4	5	6
1	A	B	C	D	E	F
2	G	H	I	J	K	L
3	M	N	O	P	Q	R
4	S	T	U	V	W	X
5	Y	Z				

The Real You!

1. How would you most want to be described?
- **a.** Funkadelic
- **b.** Elegant
- **c.** Brilliant
- **d.** Super-Stylin'

2. When you go to the salon, what do you do?
- **a.** Tell the stylist you want to be totally different than anyone she's ever worked with before. You want a look no one else has ever seen.
- **b.** Ask her for just a trim—you don't want to make any changes, since you love the way you look.
- **c.** Say, "I'd like a new cut. What do you think would work best with my hair and face?"
- **d.** Show her a picture of a model in a magazine and say, "I want to look like her."

3. If you went on a massive cleaning spree in your room, what would you find under the bed?
- **a.** Lots and lots of glitter.
- **b.** That sweater you've been searching for all month.
- **c.** The library book you forgot to return.
- **d.** Half-used make-up.

4. One of your friends gives you a blouse for your birthday that is totally not your style. What do you do?
- **a.** Wear it to school just to shake things up and surprise everyone who thinks they know you.
- **b.** Return it for something more your look.
- **c.** Wear it on a night when you and your friend are just hanging around ... alone.
- **d.** Wear it, but dress it up with lots of accessories that are more your style.

5. You go to the mall because. . .
- **a.** You need something new and hot, that no one else has got!
- **b.** You stained your white blouse and you need to replace it.
- **c.** You have a party coming up and all you have is useful, purposeful school clothes.
- **d.** Your fave boutique just got a new shipment.

6. Your dream guy is
- **a.** Stylin'—stands out from the crowd.
- **b.** Kind and polite—manners make the man.
- **c.** Smart—a dude who's more into chemistry than clothes.
- **d.** Not necessarily the cutest, but definitely the sweetest.

What kind of girl are you?

Mostly As: Guess what? You and I are very alike. In fact, I'm the girl you have the most in common with. You are totally out there, willing to take risks and go wild. You want to be noticed, and you are. Chances are you're the school trendsetter!

Mostly Bs: Have you met my buddy Cloe? She's an angel...with attitude. And so are you. You're a classic, elegant kind of girl. You are happy with who you are, and your inner peace shines through in everything you wear and do.

Mostly Cs: Like my good friend Yasmin, you're a wonderful combination of brains and beauty. You care about how you look, for sure, but you're obviously more into feeding your mind than stuffing your closet with clothes.

Mostly Ds: You should be hangin' with my bud Sasha. The two of you are always on to the newest trends before the old ones wear out. You're also both well aware that outer beauty starts with a beautiful soul.

I'm Outta Here!

There's a huge sale on silver, sparkly platform boots and I just have to be the first one there when the doors open.

The trouble is, I'm having a hard time deciding what to wear on my shopping spree. Can you come up with an outfit for this girl on the go?

Thanks! See ya' at the sale!